Rush

Of

Many

Waters

Also by Pauly Hart

Rush of Many Waters:

Volume Four

By Pauly Hart

ISBN: 978-1-955399-08-1
Library of Congress Catalog Data is available at: Loc.gov
This book is available at cost on Amazon.com and wherever
fine books are sold.
Any references to historical events, real people, or real
places are used fictitiously. Names, characters, and
places are products of the author's imagination.
Front Cover Art by Franz Marc:
Front cover design by Pauly Hart
Paperback version printed in Savannah, Georgia, USA,
where available.
First Edition, 2021
Author Contact: EmpiresAndGenerals@gmail.com
Author Website: PaulyHart.com

Contents

Shorts

The Ride

"Isaiah 13:3 from the Greek Septuagint reads this way: 'I give command, and I bring them: giants are coming to fulfil my wrath, rejoicing at the same time and insulting.'" Nathan Thompson said, and laid his phone down on the table, almost daring me to contradict him.

I sighed. "Another one?" I asked. "What will it take to prove your wrong?" I dug through the internet for a minute, going to a Strong's Concordance site and said: "A more literal interpretation of 13:3 (a) and (b) reads this way: "I have commanded the holy ones. also I have called the mighty ones to execute my anger." I looked up over my phone at him. He was putting more sugar in his coffee. "Ok, so 'Holy Ones' is 'Quadash,' which means: 'to be set apart.' That's the first word. The second word is 'Mighty Ones' or 'Gibbor,' which means: "to be strong."" He was stirring his coffee, after five more packets of sugar.

"Look, seeing as how Elohim destroyed the abominations called giants again and again, I don't believe that what you have is quality exegesis." I said, and put my phone on the table, next to his.

"So you don't believe in giants?" Nathan asked, taking a sip of his toxic brew. It was probably super-saturated with sugar, but he still grabbed the spoon and tried to crush the granules at the bottom. "You don't think that giants help build the pyramids or the Baalbek Structures?" He blew on the coffee again, taking another sip.

"I'm not saying that at all." I rolled my eyes, leaned back in the café booth chair and went into it again. "I've seen Baalbek with my own eyes man. You know I have. You know I went to Lebanon for my thesis. I had to see it for myself. I spent a year going over Urquhart's notes, and also came to no definitive conclusion. It wasn't built by Romans, that much we know."

"Yeah, I read your thesis. It was interesting." The waitress came with our meal just then, breaking away his thought pattern to the meal at hand.

"Alright guys." she said. "Veggie omelette?" I raised my hand and she set it down in front of me. "And here you go,.. Large salad." She put the bowl in front of him. "You sure you don't want any dressing?" She asked.

"Nah, I'm good." Nathan said, already tossing it around with his fork.

"Well, my name's Debbie if you need anything." she said.

"What if we don't?" I said. "Is your name still Debbie?"

She laughed. "Ah. I like that," and left us.

"Can't believe you're having a salad for breakfast." I said, a little disgusted at the idea.

"Can't believe you're eating eggs." He said. "Chickens are people too."

We left the diet issue to die mid-air, as we both attacked our breakfasts.

Almost two minutes in, Debbie came back to check on us. "Doing okay?"

We both had our mouths full, and both nodded.

"Alright. Glad you're liking it." Then she noticed my hot tea was a little low. "Need some more hot water and coffee?"

Again, we both nodded and she was off again to retrieve our drinks. Ever since I had been told of my Type 2 Diabetes, I had switched from coffee and gone to tea. I drank it with a little cream and no sugar. I couldn't stand watching Nathan do what he did to his coffee, it was so unhealthy. Here he was, a strict vegan, just pounding away on that sugar-cane. It drove me crazy.

Debbie had come and gone again, refilling our drinks and we were coming to the point in the meal where you have the choice to soldier on and finish the plate or push away the remainder and be done. I was a firm believer in getting my money's worth and cleaning my plate to not waste anything. Nathan was a firm believer in letting his body dictate when to stop eating. I suppose there was a good argument for both perspectives and since we had only known each other for a short while we didn't nit-pick with each other about the small stuff.

"So," Nathan began, wiping his face with a napkin, "You don't think that there were any giants at all? Am I missing something?"

I was scraping the remnants of my egg together and chewing thoughtfully. "No…" I began, taking time to swallow. "What I mean to say is that they're all gone and would have been gone a long time ago. The last fragments we have found of them have all been buried in history."

"What do you mean: 'buried'?" He squinted his eyes, not believing that.

I cleared my throat. "Alright. It's like this. Suppose, let's say... Just suppose... That there was a vast governmental conspiracy to cover up all the giant evidence."

"Oh here we go." He folded his arms in resignation of what he knew he was going to hear.

"Bear with me." I continued. "Now, from all of recorded history, from the petroglyphs and hieroglyphs all over Egypt, even into the late 1800's, we had evidence of them walking around building things." I put my silverware and napkin on the plate and put it towards the edge of the table, for Debbie when she came back around. Grabbing a pen from my jacket, I pulled out a napkin and began drawing.

I drew a small grid. "Each of these boxes is 5 feet, alright?" I drew a little man in the first box and a larger man in the second box and on and on to the fifth man, at twenty five feet tall. "See? OK, here is our first man in 4000 BC walking around, intermingling with these big guys. Now obviously there's more of the little guys because they eat less. But the big guys eat all the time, and they have to have a constant supply of food."

"They ate all the dinosaurs into extinction?" he asked.

"Ooooh my God." I replied, closing my eyes. "No. They *were* the dinosaurs."

"Huh?" Uncrossing his arms, he was suddenly interested.

"I'm telling you man. Just hold on. I'll get to it." I returned to my sketch. "Ok, so the little guys here are all running around, doing the bidding of these larger guys, herding sheep, growing wheat, making food for the masters of mankind. All the while, these huge guys were making these structures all over earth, man. All over. In China, in Egypt, in Mexico, in Cambodia, all over the earth. There's even some off the coasts of Cuba and The Bahamas, and even Japan. Huge pyramids all over the earth. And they all popped up about the same time."

"And Lebanon." He said, pointing to me. "Don't forget Lebanon."

"Obviously." I said, going back to my drawing. "OK, archeological records say that this second dude right here..."

"The ten footer?"

"Yeah, or thereabouts... This guy was the most pervasive of the survivors. A lot of data on these guys. Red, hairy, polydactyl, and..."

"Poly what?"

"Polydactyl. It means they have more than the normal amount of digits per appendage. Six fingers on one hand, and all that. It's why the custom in the Americas and many other places of raising the hand to show they only had five fingers." I said.

"I thought it was to show they didn't have weapons."

"Or weapons." I conceded. "But the custom was more pervasive here in the Americas than any other place. Also, in the Americas is where we have the most skulls and bones of these secondary humans. The level one giant."

"Level one giant." He thought about that for a minute. I needed to let that sink in. "So all those overly large humans with elongated heads found in South America were level one dudes."

"Exactly. They were kinda like the kings and rulers after the really big ones died off. The regular men tried to worship them and shape their heads like that too, that's why you see that a lot down there, and also in Meso-America."

"Meso?" He asked.

"Meso-America was really where a lot of the action was. It's Like Mexico down to Panama."

"Right." he said, "South America."

"North America." I looked at him sideways. "You do realize that North America is bigger than just The USA and Canada. There's twenty three countries in North America."

"Bullshit." He said.

"Whatever." I said, throwing up my hands. "I'm gonna take a leak, you look it up." I got up and went to the restroom.

When I came back Nathan had already paid and was standing by the table, Coffee Go-cup in hand.

"Ready?" he asked, and started walking toward the door. I took a long look at the toast I hadn't eaten and decided that discretion was the better part of a Diabetic diet. I threw down a five dollar bill and grabbed my napkin diagram.

"Yuppers."

We walked to the van parked in the handicapped spot. On the side of the bright blue van was a huge diagram of the Gleeson Azimuthal Projection "Flat Earth" map. It was decorated with stickers and Bible verses to support its claims. He jingled the keys, hit the fob and unlocked it.

Getting in, I remembered how I had met this character, just days ago at the Flat Earth Convention here in Dallas. He had invited me to stay after, and I changed my plans and stayed with him for a couple of days. We got in and he started the van up.

"Okay. So we got these level zero humans and these level one giants ruling over them, telling them what to do… What about the bigger ones? Where do they fit in?" He began, pulling out into the parking lot, looking for an opening to exit the strip-mall.

"Alright, now from what I understand, around 2,345 BC the great deluge knocked them all out." I started, ready to continue the enlightenment of my new friend.

"Great deluge? Noah's flood?" he asked, pulling into traffic.

"Correct. And so we know from Egyptian glyphs that all the bigger ones died off. Every one of them. As a matter of fact, anything that wasn't on the ark died. The only human survivors were of this smaller type. Noah wasn't defiled by the first Archon incursion, nor were his sons. It couldn't have been Noah's wife, so it had to have been one of the son's wives."

"One of what?" he laughed, coming to a stop light.

"One of the giant's DNA must have been latent in the wives of Noah's sons. One of them, or all of them, must have had some latent DNA for the giant kind, because after the great deluge, there are no great buildings ever again. They all happened before the great deluge."

"Like Cahokia?" he asked.

"Ah, you're on it now." I said, holding up a hand for a high-five. No high-five came, so I looked over at him.

He was looking at the side mirror. "You see that black Denali behind us?" He asked, distracted.

I turned around in my seat. Looking through the van's back windows was a new black Denali, with black trim. "What about it?" I asked.

"It was in the parking lot earlier too." I looked concerned.

I laughed. "You think it's following us?"

"Stranger things have happened bro. Much stranger things."

The light turned green, and he turned right, with no signal. Sure enough, the car followed us.

A couple of seconds went by and he seemed over the idea of being followed. He cleared his throat and said: "Alright. So before Noah builds the ark, or before it floods or whatever, these giants were walking around doing whatever they wanted? They were just builders and mad-men?"

"Well, yeah. Imagine all these bigger guys running around doing whatever they wanted. No one could tell them no. They would just step on you if you tried to fight against them. Nobody could stop them, I think that's why Elohim wiped them all out. They were false elohim. They were the monsters of whom stories were told. That's Genesis 6:4 right after He cursed their years.

"Cursed their years?" Nathan asked.

"Yeah, Genesis 6:3 says he limited their lifespan to 120 years. Cause before that, they were living up to a thousand years."

"Nimrod ruled for 500 years though." Nathan said.

"True. But he was Noah's great-grandson. It must have taken some time for the curse to take effect. It wasn't an overnight thing. He's a merciful God. But, while we're on the topic, look at Nimrod, he must have been one of the larger ones, because he banded a bunch of them together and tried to outdo a lot of the older buildings. And this was years after the flood. All those ancient monoliths and pyramids were either covered up or flooded… He wanted to bring back the good old days."

"And reach heaven." Nathan added.

"Correct. He defied Elohim, setting himself up to be his own elohim, and defied the Creator Elohim Yahway."

"Damn." Nathan added. "They're still back there. Good thing I'm packing."

I swallowed. "Packing? You're carrying a gun?"

He looked at me with a strange smile. "Sure I am. I've got two in the van right now. You know how to shoot?"

I put my hands up. "I'm not shooting anyone."

He frowned. "Fine," and pulled into McDonalds, veering for the drive thru lane.

"You going to see what they do?" I asked, a little nervous.

Without answering, he put the car into park in the drive thru line and got out, reaching under the seat as he did, pulling out a Glock 19. He tucked it into the small of his back, in his pants. The Denali had pulled in behind us in the drive thru, but when they saw Nathan coming, they reversed and spun out, then shot out of the parking lot onto the street and raced from view.

"Yeah, run away chicken!" He was screaming at them.

He got back in the van, put the gun under the seat, backed out of the drive thru and followed after them. They had a pretty good head start, and Nathan obeyed the traffic laws, so they got away pretty quickly. We drove a little way down the road until he spotted a cemetery entrance, slowed and took it.

"A cemetery?" I thought to myself. Well, it did make sense. Here we were in a bright blue van, with "Join the Flat Earth Revolution" painted on the outside of it. I guess this would be one of those places where no one would bother you.

He was still fuming. Turning off the van, he adjusted his seat and looked at me, dead on.

"Alright bro. Either they don't like the fact that I'm with you, or they've finally decided to get rid of me." He said it slowly, weighing his words. "Either way, it's bad news for you too."

"You know who they are?" I asked timidly.

"Someone in the D.O.D."

"Department of Defense?" I asked slowly.

"Yeah, someone like that. I can't be sure." he said, then confided. "They do this a lot. They follow me and then run away. But this is the first time I've seen an official unmarked on me."

I laughed. "Maybe it was the Smithsonian."

He laughed too. "What? Why would they send the Smithsonian after me?"

I suddenly wasn't laughing. What if it was?

"Um." I began. "Because they're behind the cover-up of the giants in the first place."

He squinted his eyes. "Go on. I'm all ears."

"They were the ones who stole all the giant bones and reorganized them into the dinosaurs."

"Yeah, you were saying that earlier in the restaurant." He moved around, almost facing me in the drivers' seat.

"So right." I began. "Somewhere around the mid 1800's, when newspapers were really taking off and when industrialization really took hold of the U.S.A., people were finding and reporting huge bones from beings up to twenty five feet tall. Sometimes even larger, though these are harder to prove. But it was in May of 1846 that the Smithsonian started being built by President James Polk. He was a Democrat and Freemason and called for "Westward Expansion" the idea built around: "Manifest Destiny." The white man, in the form of the United States government must finish subduing the natives, finish subduing the British, and kick out the French, the Spanish, the Dutch, and the Mexicans. It was a big deal."

"Manifest Destiny." He thought about it.

"Right. Polk brainwashed citizens into believing it was their spiritual duty to kill the other races. They even made paintings about it, showing huge angels and the hand of God guiding the way west. Like the Israelites in Canaan." I said.

"And the Smithsonian was... What?" he asked.

"Curators of the unknown. 'To spread and diffuse knowledge.' They used the name of a deceased English chemist and his gift of land to the government to start their capture of all things mysterious. And was it any surprise that in 1842, Richard Owen came along and said: "These bones aren't from the monsters of the Bible, but from a new race of animals called: 'Terrible lizards' – that's 'deinos and sauros' in Latin... 'Dinosaur.'"

"They turned all the giant bones into dino bones? How did they do it? I've seen a dinosaur exhibit, and there's no way some of those could have been men."

"Skeletal structures often disappoint, I'm afraid. Remember Egyptian hieroglyphs, how some of their largest gods had features of other animals? You think that's coincidence that they would find a huge malformed head that could have been one of those dead Egyptian gods and just move a couple of things around and call them something else?"

He didn't say anything, but had begun chewing his lip, deep in concentration.

"And do you think that they want anyone ruining their plans? With giant bones, they can only point to the Bible as truth, but with Dinosaur bones, they can point to Darwinian Evolution as truth."

It was then that four black Denalis pulled into the cemetery.

As they grew closer, I could make out the black on black stencil that ran the length of the front doors. 'Smithsonian National Museum of Natural History.'

Juggling

Nick thought the best part of the funeral was the food. Sure, you had to get past the lines of grievers, but once you did, you got to eat for free. Mr. Cornish's funeral reception was no different. Oh sure he knew Teddy Cornish. Nick found the obituary and then an old microfiche at the library had some of his classmates and he was a passing likeness for "Jim Ebernat."

Funerals were easy. Nick hit one or two a day. So he had attended and eaten the food and stolen a little money here and there and then was out the door. Except for the dark man following him. Around the corner, to the parking lot.

The man grabs Nick and shoves him up against a burgundy SUV. "You juggling'?" The dark man asks.

"What the heck is that?" Nick asks, wide eyed.

The dark man looks left and then right and then leans in real close. "I found your marker," and holds up a business card with a "ϕɤ" on it. Nick is horrified and confused and has no idea what that card could be and tells the dark man as much.

Just then, from beside them both, a long gun appeared at the dark man's head. It was attached to a rather normal looking arm and a normal looking man, who said very quietly: "That's my card."

"You're the juggler?" The dark man asked, not turning his head or releasing Nicks collar.

"Indubitably." The juggler said.

"Then who the hell is this?" The dark man asked.

"I have no idea." The juggler said, and shot Nick in the head.

"I believe we have some business then." The dark man said, letting Nick sink to the ground on the side of the SUV.

The Goforth

Kwazzil was four foot three and made of Rubber Bands. At least, that's what his wrestling coach told him.

"Rubber Band Man!" He would yell, "Go show them how it's done!"

And Kwazzil would run out there and pin his opponent in three seconds. That's how it was done, and he did it every time. He didn't warm up. Not really, anyway. He did a lot of extra stretches, while the other guys on the team were doing burpees. Back and forth and back and forth... He would still be there on the sidelines, stretching away.

"Why... Doesn't... Rubber run... with... us?" Todd asked, out of breath when the team was all done with warm-up.

"Because he doesn't need to." Chuck, the coach, smiled. "He's my golden boy."

So the Jay High School Royals Seniors and Juniors would pair off and go to the mats while the Junior-Varsity would go through some extra training. It was Kwazzil's third year on varsity, something that was rare, but not unheard of. This was his Senior year. He had taken state as a JV starter. He had been the only JV to go to state, and honestly, he had led them all the way. It had been so easy for him.

He had been wrestling with his dad since before he could walk. It hadn't really been planned, his dad said, it had just kept up that way. As soon as dad got home, they would go at it. The children of Bulgarian immigrants, they were proud of their heritage, and part of that was wrestling. Over the years, they had built a ring out in the yard, then during winter they moved it into the garage. Mom would officiate and Kwazzil's little brother Zumzi would get to ring the bell. Somewhere around thirteen, Kwazzil had started beating his dad... And he hadn't lost since. He hadn't grown either. At four foot three inches he was pretty short for a high-schooler and he was extremely short for a senior. He used it to his advantage.

It wasn't that he was bulky. He wasn't. He wasn't really skinny either. He was average for what you expected from his height, albeit, the height of a child. His brother, Zumzi was now in the eighth grade and was almost a head taller than him. Zumzi didn't wrestle. He had tried to, but he was horrible at it. His big thing was online gaming. And, although he loved it, he was an average player. No e-sports tournaments for him. The family faced the truth: Kwazzil was the blessed one.

So it wasn't really a surprise when Rogers State University visited with their team, to spar specifically with Kwazzil. They brought in their top five wrestlers, from all classes, just to see what kid was made of. The rest of the Royals got to spectate.

Wham! The first one went down. Wham! The second one was just as fast. The third guy weighed 164 and it took a couple of seconds to get him. Kwazzil still weighed an even 99, which was why when the fourth guy came up, he hesitated. College heavyweight class started at 183 pounds. This guy looked around 250. That was scary. Plus, he had a full beard and tattoos.

"Let's see what you got, little man." the man said, rolling his neck and shrugging his shoulders. He didn't have to wait long though. Kwazzil used a double leg takedown with a twist and the man fell flat on his face.

"Ru-bber! Ru-bber!" His teammates roared as Kwazzil snaked behind him for a cradle. The big man, chagrined, sat back down with his teammates. It was time for the last challenger. He didn't look like much of a fighter, more like someone with an aging disease. When he took off his sweats, his red and blue Hillcats unitard didn't reveal any snake-like muscles. His arms and legs were dark and skinny... And he was super hairy. He didn't have any serious bulk though, somewhere around the 135 mark maybe... But he seemed more than confident. He kept his head down, but you could tell that he was even smiling.

"Coach, this is Micah." He gestured at him. "He's from Pakistan or somewhere like that. We got him this semester." The college coach spoke to Kwazzil's coach, Chuck, like they were old friends. Maybe they were. Kwazzil had no way of knowing. The Pakistani wrestler smiled a very tiny smile and extended his hand toward Kwazzil, who reached for it, to shake. Maybe it was the static off the mats, but their fingers zapped when they touched - a blue arc of miniaturized lightning.

The Pakistani's eyes grew very large and he became almost reverent.

He didn't say anything, oddly, but bowed very low, eyes closed. It was a little awkward at first but then suddenly   Micah grabbed Kwazzil by the shoulders, hugged him, and sniffed his hair. Kwazzil pulled away quickly. Woah, that was weird.

The College coach laughed. "Hey Mike! Don't get all mushy!" he said to the wrestler. "Get out there and show us what you got."

The college coach looked sideways at Kwazil's coach and then said: "He don't speak at all, a weird little fellow, but he sure can bring me medals."

Coach Chuck clapped his hands loudly. "Let's wrastle!" he roared, over pronouncing the "a" sound. He was an Okie to the bone.

Micah nodded and came forward. Through that huge nose of his, he was taking really deep, long breaths. In... Out... He got into position.

Micah was either really hairy or prematurely bald, Kwazzil couldn't tell. The halo of long peach fuzz surrounding his head and face was matched by the same blonde hair all over his body. It was a strange contrast with his dark skin. His nose was huge and he had a full beard, but it was the same odd peachy fuzzy hair that covered his whole body, not the black beard you would think of someone from Southern Asia. Underneath his massive nose was something like a tiny mouth.

"What an unfortunate looking dude." Kwazzil noted to himself, but didn't have much time to dwell on it because it went off. Round and round, Kwazzil reaching in, Micah getting out. Micah spinning in, Kwazzil (true to his nick-name) bouncing away. At the end, no one had any firm grapples or takedowns. Neither one had even come close.

"Again!" The College coach yelled. And so they went back at it. Except this time, Micah did a reversal and got Kwazzil in close.

In wrestling, your heads come close often. One of these times, Micah breathed into Kwazzil's ear. Wheeze in. Wheeze out. What the hell? This guy made Kwazzil super uncomfortable. Distracted, Micah took his opportunity. With a crack, Micah was on top, pinning Kwazzil. It was almost like he had some unseen arms that snaked out and grabbed him. That was impossible. Was his hair helping him somehow? That was insane... But here Kwazzil was, being pinned.

The count went out - Micah had won.

The high school team was silent. They had never seen Kwazzil, The Rubber Band Man, lose. The college team was silent as well. Secretly they had been hoping for the high school wonder to put the freak in his place. Even if he was on their team. None of them liked the immigrant. Even the coach didn't trust him. It went past the ugly factor of his weird hair and face, something about him was off, but you couldn't put your finger on it.

That night, Kwazzil couldn't sleep, and when he did, it would be Micah's face whispering to him.

"Release..." he would hiss.

Kwazzil would wake up in a cold sweat.

This happened night after night. Micah's face, whispering.

A week later, on Saturday, Micah rang his doorbell. It was mid-afternoon and he had ridden all the way from Claremore on a mountain bike. That was a four hour ride.

He marveled at this. Micah just waved his hand, and pointed to his bike. "Ride?" He breathed, mopping his sweat with the bottom of his shirt. He pointed at his bike and motioned to Kwazzil, then to the garage.

"Uh... Yeah! Hold on!" Kwazzil said and ran to the garage from inside the kitchen. In a minute he was out the back door on his bike. If this dude wanted to ride, Kwazzil was up for it. He loved his bike.

Micah pointed to his own clothes and then to Kwazzils. Kwazzil looked down at his jeans and nodded. Micah was wearing shorts and a loose T-shirt. He didn't wait for Kwazzil to respond. "Water?" Micah gestured, and Kwazzil brought him in through the open front door to the kitchen.

"Uh, yeah!" he said, "In there!" Kwazzil raced up the stairs to his room to change.

When Kwazzil came back down wearing jeans and a T-shirt, Micah was leaning over the kitchen island with a small towel. He wet it in the sink and rubbed it over his head, arms, neck and legs. Kwazzil thought that maybe he should have shown him to the bathroom instead.

He waited until Micah had finished. Micah smiled, clapped his hands and motioned to go outside. He got on the bike and took off, motioning for Kwazzil to follow.

The ride was fast. Micah didn't say much but there would have been no way for Kwazzil to respond - the speed was so fast that Kwazzil didn't have time to think. Even if he had, Micah's pace was insane, and he was so far ahead that he didn't know if he would hear him. They were dodging left and right, going down 5th street like madmen, south, out of town. They took the country road twists and turns with insane speed and terrorized squirrels and raccoons alike. Kwazzil had never ridden so fast on these roads before. Not on his own, and not with anyone else. With Micah setting the pace, and him being forced to keep up, it was one of the largest rushes he had experienced in his life.

Once in a while, a car would whiz past them, spewing up dust as it was forced to pass them using the shoulder. Other than that, the roads were mostly empty. When the driver of a white 90's Dodge truck had thrown a beer can at them, it didn't surprise Kwazzil. Nobody biked these roads. His mom's friend Traci, had been in a wreck down here last year. With all the twists and turns, you could go off into a hollow (Okies pronounced it "holler") pretty easily.

They went on several miles until they came to Eucha Lake. "Eucha" was written this way, but everyone he had ever known called it "Oochie." It was named after a famous Cherokee chief and that's how they said it, so that's how everyone said it. Though no one liked bikers, Eucha still had some of the best paths in the area. Micah slowed considerably and sat up, letting his arms and back rest. Kwazzil pulled up beside him and did the same. After the break-neck pace of the country road, the hypnotic pace had been broken by Micah's sudden let-up. They went up on 4600 towards where Brush Creek had its spill-off into the lake. It was nice. His legs appreciated the slow-down. They were burning.

"Why so slow?" Kwazzil asked.

Micah smiled his small smile and looked at Kwazill. Turning left on the road by the river, there were some trails towards the creek lagoon, and Micah took them.

Kwazzil followed. It was bumpy and rough and they started going down the bank towards the river run-off. He swallowed his spit but kept his wheel pointed down. At the bottom, Micah shifted gears all the way to the top and started pedaling like a madman.

"Sand!" Kwazzil yelled, but it was too late. He hit the bank and bottomed out. He had to get off and push.

Micah shook his head and did something like laughter, but he didn't make any noise, he was already at the top of the first bank before it hit the water.

Kwazzil, ashamed of disappointing his weird new college friend, rammed his bike to the top of the mound then came down the other side.

Before the creek bed was a small sandy shoreline with not much going on except for a few gull turds and zebra mussel shells. Micah was using a long branch to clean up an area about twice the size of a wrestling ring. With the branch, in the packed sand, he drew the actual ring out but didn't connect the line. First he very carefully inspected it for live creatures like sand spiders or mussels. Seeing none, he gestured to Kwazzil.

Kwazzil stepped in the ring and then Micah drew the circle closed, with himself inside, and threw the branch out.

"Now I kill you." Micah said, and smiled broadly.

There was a pause.

"Wait. What?" Kwazzil said.

Still smiling his weird smile, Micah started taking off his shirt. Then his shoes, his socks, and then his shorts. He wasn't wearing any underwear. Naked, Micah looked at Kwazzil and pointed at his clothes. His back and chest had the same weird patchy bald fuzzy hair all over it.

"Great, I'm at the beach with a perv who just told me he was going to kill me." Kwazzil thought to himself.

"I want to go home." he told Micah.

Micah laughed and did a somersault, then a forward breakfall left, then right, throwing himself around like a madman, after five more flips and lands, he looked up at Kwazzil. It was like he was enjoying Kwazzil squirm. He crouched on all fours and motioned to him.

"Come on." Micah said.

There was no way he was going to wrestle a naked college perv. And still, they didn't have footgear or headgear. They were hot, sweaty, and gross. Kwazzil didn't want to grapple with this guy here or now or any time in the future. But he didn't want to freak Micah out about taking all his clothes off, so Kwazzil tried to blame it on the sand.

"Aw come on man." he said, gesturing lamely around them. "We're gonna get all sandy."

The smile from Micah's face dissolved and he dove for Kwazzil's legs. It was like a switch had flipped. Micah dove for him and brought him down, only for Kwazzil to wriggle out of the hold. It was on. Round and round they went. Diving for good holds, getting in and then escaping. Rubber Band Man was really living up to his name. He had forgotten about Micah being naked and was going for the win each moment.

For a long time, neither one was coming up ahead. No holds were being kept. This went for long time, Kwazzil put his hand up.

"Time!" Putting his hands on his hips he leaned back to face the sky, stretching his back. Not a cloud in the sky, it was getting hotter.

"I need a drink." Kwazzil said.

As he tried to leave the circle, he found he could not. Coming to the edge of the circle, where the sand line had been drawn, a wave of dizziness came over him and he fell over.

Kwazzil shook it off and tried again. Nothing could get him over the line. Trembling, he moved on all fours only to vomit within inches of the line.

"W-what?" he shuttered.

Micah walked to him slowly. He gently touched the border of the drawn circle and a light green shimmer flowed in and around his hand, as if he were touching a jade puddle.

"This is your end." Micah said. "Only if you beat me, you escape." His eyes were dark, mingled with the knowledge of a hunter who has ensnared his prey. He was above Kwazzil and looked down on him as he spoke. Kwazzil could see all the way up his nose, but under his nose, he couldn't see his mouth.

Wait. What? Kwazzil slowly stood up, keeping his eyes on Micah's mouth the whole time. Being dizzy, he had to use Micah to stand, and as he came face to face with him, Micah lifted his chin up and rubbed his hand over his mouth, only to move the mouth an inch to the left. It was... It was not a mouth at all. It had been makeup, or some sort of marker.

Micah had no mouth.

"W-wh-wha…" Kwazzil stuttered and fell back down again. "How? H-w-what?" He stammered again. "You don't have a mouth." he said to Micah.

Micah squatted and leaned over him. His peachy fuzzy hair, glistening in the air, moved on its own, though there was no wind. He peered into Kwazzil's eyes and said.

"To become stronger. To prepare body for long-life. To live forever. I kill you now." Micah smiled broadly. His cheek muscles brought up to his face, but at the slit where everyone else had teeth and a tongue, Micah had just more skin and hair. To Kwazzil, he looked like a shark. Then he stopped smiling, reared down and said in a low whisper: "Fight."

"H-how are you even talking to me right now?!" Kwazzil yelled at him, not getting up.

"Mind-speak." Micah told him, and tapped his temple.

Kwazzil was furious. "This naked college perv wants to kill me and eat me. This… This… freak… With no mouth wants to eat me? What kind of monster is this? No. Not today boy. Not today." He readied himself for Micah's attack.

He knew he would come hard and fast, and he was ready. he took off his shirt, and placing it on the ground, he grabbed a handful of sand. Micah sprang. Kwazzil threw the sand as hard as he could into his face and Micah rolled away, clawing at his eyes. Kwazzil rolled to where Micah had put his other clothes, looking for a belt or something to use as a weapon. Nothing.

Micah came at him and threw him to the ground and grappled him. His arms were snakes, and he was fast. Kwazzil, using every trick in the book now, dirty or not, punched him in the groin hard. Micah went down and Kwazzil, the Rubber Band Man, was on his back with his T-shirt, around his throat.

This was no longer wrestling. This was survival. There had to be some way of gaining the upper hand. Kwazzil pulled the shirt as tight as he could, hoping to knock him unconscious, or make him lose his breath, or something. Micah's big nose started making snorting noises, a good sign that he was having trouble. Micah rolled forward and launched Kwazzil away and threw the T-shirt out of the ring. Quick as a whip, Micah reached his own clothes and threw them out too.

Micah glowered, rubbing his weird groin and tiny penis, covered in that weird and tiny hair. Micah was mad. Maybe he would make a mistake. Micah launched for his legs but Kwazzil leapt up and tried to come down on his back but mistimed it. Kwazzil fell flat on his chest. Micah was on him in an instant.

Kwazzil was face down in the sand on his chest and Micah was on his back like a leech. Kwazzil tried an elbow to the face but missed. Micah's right arm snaked through Kwazzil's left arm and with his right hand over his back, Micah grabbed his right wrist. The arm bar. Kwazzil cursed himself for being so stupid. This was almost impossible to get out of. He kicked up his legs to try to regain support but Micah was too strong.

The sand pushed up in Kwazzil's face and Micah kept moving forward, trapping Kwazzil's arms in and driving Kwazzil sideways and into control. As before, it felt like tiny tentacles moving up and down on him, forcing him to do Micah's bidding. The hair all over his body seemed to help bring Kwazzil into submission.

It was over. Kwazzil was stuck. Micah's hair was in Kwazzil's mouth, his nose, his eyes. As Micah firmed up the hold and pushed Micah deeper and deeper into the sand, Kwazzil's shoulders were stuck fast and his face was brought upwards into the chest and armpit of Micah's left arm. The stench from the armpit was overwhelming, as it ground itself deeper and deeper into his face.

What went through Kwazzil's mind last was the strange sounds of Micah inhaling deeply through his nose, deeper and deeper. He was smelling him with that huge nose of his. All nose and no mouth. Wheeze in. Wheeze out.

The sound reminded him of the ocean.

Poems

Army girl in her closet

Where are the valleys filled with flowers?
Where are the mountains with snow?
Where are the meadows, where are the children?
I sure wish, I'd like to know.

Where is the laughter, where is the singing?
Where are the people who care?
Where is the villa with bells that are ringing?
I would like to go.

I want to be where the happiness is.
I wish we all could be fine.
I wonder why good people die?
I'm sure that I don't know.

Why are you crying, why are you hurting?
Talk with me to the end.
Please don't be lonely, please don't be dying.
Please don't be hurting, please don't be crying.
I want to go where the children are playing.
Take me there, take me there.
Take me there, my friend.

'Twas Luck

A bread crumb fell on a path
Forgotten by a weary travelers purse
and perchance lay in a sunlit way
spied by a lark on a perch.

As the bird would have
he did take to his wing
lighting upon bread in a swoop
and catching it up in his beak

But luck is cruel this fateful day
for at this time a cat a prowl
not a sound nor a fray
could help this lark that day

                              If you say something

"If you say something

    loud enough
    often enough

People are

    simple enough

to believe that
they can have

    more than enough

of what you have

    little enough of."

                              they are back

caged in a thousand tons of granite

they came long far ago
they been here ever since
chained
bound
and
enslaved

wracking their souls for freedom

they came long time ago
they be here long time now
screaming
writhing
and
imprisoned

listening to you sleep

they wake now from the graves
wanting to feed again
seething
searching
and
enfleshed
listening to you cry

demon nephilim
calling out
through the
pentagram
of your minds
third eye

listening to you pray

demon nephilim
calling your name

calling your name
to do their bidding
and join them
in hell

                                              To fly

Isn't it wonderful?
A bird flies.
A crow cries,
and all my life just dies,
as Christ lives,
and I give,
and all my gifts seem despised.
As I kill, then He will,
and He fills
me up each day.
My soul flies,
and my spirit within
does rise.
Just as I am
without one plea,
but that His blood was shed for me.

            The confrontation of conniption.

what you can gain in a lifetime

        you can lose in a moment

what you can see in the morning

        you can lose in the night

what someone can talk you into

    some one can talk you out of

and what you can accept in emotion

    you can lose in logic

                                  Cry

The cry of my heart
Is to love you
Though I go through very hell itself

It's the cry of my heart
To worship you
To love you like nobody else

Though many trials may come my way
I know this one thing stays the same
You are forever lovely true

And I will trust in you

                       Spontaneous Psalm #11

Holy Spirit come and fill this cup today
Holy Spirit come and fill this cup today
Blessed Savior show us you're the only way
Blessed Jesus come and fill our lives today

You are holy
Holy Messiah
Holy Lord

And we walk in one accord

Oh fill our cup today
Holy Spirit come down when we pray
To the Father

Fill us Holy Father
Fill us Holy Father

Let us rejoice in you!
Do something Lord Jesus!

When I'm tired I will turn to you
When I'm tired, you have the strength
To pull me through
You are my joy

You are my joy and my salvation

Essays

Breaking the Big Buddy Chain

Oh Texas. What a wonderful country in and of itself. My father and mother's siblings all still lived in Texas. All the grandparents and cousins and nephews and uncles and aunts all lived in Texas. But all my kin were big time Masons who ran the Northern Chihuahua desert. My immediate family had escaped to Kansas, by way of a round-the-world trip... But back to Texas my mom and I went. I was fifteen and on fire for Jesus. I wanted to go hear the great Big Buddy Belcher teach me how to be even more on fire for Jesus. Dallas, Texas was home of many Charismatic Institutions. If Wichita had the Holy Spirit at one fold, and Tulsa at five fold, then Dallas surely had it at twenty five fold. At least, this is how my youthful mind perceived things.

"Health and Wealth" churches were everywhere. And it all hinged on "FAITH." I was poor because I lacked faith. I was sick because I lacked faith. Even though the doctors had proclaimed on me the pronouncement of four individual "Spontaneous Remissions" I still had health issues. Prune Belly Syndrome had robbed me of all my stomach muscles. With no abdominal muscles, only my skin remained to hold in my organs. I looked pregnant or fat or like one of the "Ethiopian Children" that Sally Struthers showed me on TV. Deformity had been depressing. When all of your friends make fun of you, do you really have friends?

So we were there at Big Buddy's to seek more healing. My mom likened us to the woman who had reached out to grab Jesus' tzitzits, and be healed from the issue of blood. She said we needed faith, and that we couldn't let God show our fear, but we had to have faith, faith, faith. And so the service went. Me, drawing tiny creatures and monsters and space battles on my little tablet until the sermon was over and the altar call had begun.

I don't know what the altar call was for... It could have been for anything. The old joke in Charismania went something like this –

"The preacher winds up the sermon and has everyone close their eyes and bow their heads. Then he asks people to stand up if they are battling depression or have lost a job or are praying for their children to come back to the Lord... Obviously many people stand up. Then he asks if they would also stand if they are battling homosexuality and then has everyone open their eyes. The seated gaze upon the standing who seem to be battling homosexuality but really stood up for depression."

Whatever the altar call was for, we went down the aisle to the front to be prayed for. My mom, also not in the greatest of health, lived for moments like this. She had come out of the "Jesus Movement" of the '70's, and loved that old timey "Kumbuya Moment." I was there for results. None of that touchy-feely stuff for me thanks. I had a job contract that needed order fulfilment. Healing. Now. Post-haste.

Big Buddy came by, laid his hands on my mom's head and shouted: "TOUCH!" and did the same to me. "TOUCH!" and shimmied on by, a wisp in the spotlight.

We lingered a little bit. My mom, crying and standing there, as I watched Big Buddy walk down the line saying the same thing to everyone else. Once he reached the end, he exited stage left. A shill for the spotlight. I looked down around me at the (mostly) women who had come up to be prayed over by the "Man of God." There were "Lap Blanket People" walking around, laying tiny blankets on the end of women's skirts and over men's groins. There was soft music playing. There were a few people left in the seating area "Basking in the Anointing" and that was it.

These people were here for an emotional experience. I didn't feel like Jesus had even come in the room.

It was sad.

Nothing happened and we went home.

The Lord, evidently, was not impressed with either our "FAITH" or Big Buddy Belcher's.

And I say that a little tongue-in-cheek. Obviously God loved us. But the tangible evidence of the Holy Spirit of God, as evidenced by me in many other prayer meetings, was not present. It was a song and a dance and five cents from France.

I made a small vow that if I ever went into the ministry full time, I wouldn't have a ministry like Big Buddy Belcher's. Rather, I would take Jesus to the people, like, well... Like Jesus would have.

Captivity freed in death

How it fully seems to be the beginning of my life. I see and hear and smell and taste all there is despite... my captivity, which now seems like a welcome thing compared to the death I must face before I am freed. "I'm Human!" I scream! But it's just a blur, a kick in yearning. They won't listen, they are deafened with reason, lies, hate. They don't see me for who I am. They don't and they won't. But, I still love them. I don't love them for what they do, but rather, for who they are. I just don't understand? Why can't I be free like they are? I'm innocent! I've never faced a jury for my alleged crimes! Crimes? The only crime I've committed is my existence! I'm not a criminal, I'm an offering. A ritual sacrifice in the name of convenience and in the name of free choice. You see, I may be young, but I've got choice too! But no one can hear me. I am powerless in this struggle. Because if my mother chooses death for me, I can't refuse. I love her. Who am I to say that she's wrong? I only wish she loved me too. I'm a part of her! But she's much wiser than I.

But oh, how I covet the life of the free! They say that life is a fragrance, smelt and then gone. No one has smelled me. I should be a flower. But I'm a forgotten weed. Someone nobody wants to think about. Why God? Why? I know you love me! Don't you? Oh please don't turn your back on me too! I know that no one really hates me... Thy are just confused, mixed up. Things may not be well with me, but they can always get better with them! Where's my daddy? I wish I could see his face... I want to thank him for this small glimpse of life he has given me. I love him. I just don't understand... I guess

I must have done something wrong. I've been bad. I'm sorry. I really am. I tried to be good, but I guess I wasn't.

I love you. Goodbye.

Who am I?

If I dream, I dream of Loneliness. I sit hollow, doubtless I die inside. My world is hollow and my hands are numb from holding deaths frozen door. I am an empty shell of a lost spectre. Women see me as shy. Bothersome. They don't perceive. And they don't care. I could spend my whole life emptying myself and pouring out my soul to the world and yet none would catch even a glimpse of the beginnings of me. What does my life amount to? Who knows? Who actually cares anyway? My voice is the lost voice of reason in a lusty wrangle with the great kiss of passion. For logic is but a beggar, crying out raw at the doorway of emotion. Clinging... Always clinging. Am I Solomon? Does my life equal his vision and meaninglessness? My knowledge is equal to that of a god, by my actions betray my unrighteous and meager existence. Mouths ramble in front of me, speaking tunnel-visioned idealisms, missing the point. MISSING THE WHOLE POINT! I am alone in my wisdom. For my wisdom is not of this world. It is divine. But divinity enfleshed is an elusive creature. A very hard subject to grasp. So, when I dream, I dream of a day where Martin Luther and Martin Luther King Jr. stand side by side and chant the very oracles of Jehovah. They preach? Yes. They preach, but who is there to listen? Yellow, spineless I. I hear but do not act upon suppositions given by martyrs. These words haunt me. Is my life more or is it less than the sum of my actions? Where does the fulcrum sit in my decrepit philosophy? I don't understand. I can't understand any more than I do. Why? Why? Why in Gods' holy name can't I be strong? Like my mentors before me? Like St. Paul, like Elijah, like Josiah, like Jesus? Jesus was so perfect... So much like His Father in Heaven. He was one with his Father. My goal then, is typified in him. How can I even begin to fathom His likeness, when my very own likeness is a dead shadow that is formless in a world that is wrinkled and black. Taste and smell evade me. Taste is tasteless and pain is never painless. Every summation of my hypothetical life add up to this: I can not do what I say. I do not do what is right to do, and do not care to either. Therein lies the problem. A very serious problem. But this problem is not seen by others. For others babble like brooks. And, as I sit, alone in my canoe, I hear them. I don't listen, but instead, paddle the other way.

Summer Camp Salvation

Summertime for a child is a landscape open to the imagination. Nothing is too large, nothing is impossible, nothing is out of reach. At least it felt that way in uptown Wichita in the early eighties. Summertime is also Summer Camp time, and that's where the magic happens. And no, I'm not talking about where you got your first French kiss. I'm talking about that time where there was some really cool music playing and you heard a really cool testimony and you raised your hand when the preacher asked you if you wanted to be a missionary for the rest of your life. That time.

And from age eight until I was sixteen I either visited Summer Camp or worked at Summer Camp. Omega Ranch, Harvest Christian and the Wichita YMCA. It was at these places that I learned how to take my book knowledge and turn it into actuality. It was at Omega Ranch that I found God in all things and learned how to hear his voice. At Harvest Christian, I learned how to put his words into practice and at the YMCA I learned how to share what I had learned with people who didn't know Jesus firsthand. Summer Camp changed my life.

When I was sixteen I worked at Harvest Christian. At that time it was pretty small and was only open for four weeks. The first week I worked in the kitchen as a dishwasher, the second week I mowed lawns and dumped trash barrels, the third week I was a counselor and the fourth week they let me actually attend the camp as a camper. The third week was awesome because me and my eight year old crew spent the week in a tipi. Wait, except for that time that it monsooned and drenched all of our luggage and clothes. At any rate, we had fun. But it was the fourth week that really stirred up my hunger for the truths of the Bible and the larger scope of who God really was.

I didn't give them any money for being a camper on week four, but then again, they didn't pay me for the first three weeks either. That was fair. And that fourth week though. Being able to experience the horseback riding and swimming and crafting and Bible studies that all the other campers had experienced, being able to relax after all that hard work? Wow. It was the most fulfilling reward for work experience in my short sixteen years on earth. But as great as the days were at Harvest Christian, the night services were even better. Now, I don't know how much you want to believe in an active and working God, but I was witness to physical healings and divine miracles. The most notable was a girl who, in the middle of a very quiet moment in service screamed out: "I can see! I can see!" She had been born with eyesight so bad that it required her to wear glasses almost an inch thick.

Night services were sometimes so powerful that they would often last until midnight. Nothing like singing until your voice is raw in worship to the Creator of the earth. My heart overflowed with a pure devotion so large that I couldn't contain any sin in my life any longer. And I took this awesome presence of mind home. It was right before my Junior year in high school (grade 11) and I was out to make a change in my life. I was going to harken to the calling of God on my heart. I was going to effect change in my world. I would be a missionary for Him, I would follow Him only, and I would burn all of my comic books.

www.ingramcontent.com/pod-product-compliance
Lightning Source LLC
Chambersburg PA
CBHW030153200626
46812CB00016B/1822